Acting Edition

You Can See All The Stars

by E. M. Lewis

FOR PRODUCTION INQUIRIES

UNITED STATES AND CANADA
info@concordtheatricals.com
1-866-979-0447

UNITED KINGDOM AND EUROPE
licensing@concordtheatricals.co.uk
020-7054-7298

Each title is subject to availability from Concord Theatricals Corp., depending upon country of performance. Please be aware that *YOU CAN SEE ALL THE STARS* may not be licensed by Concord Theatricals Corp. in your territory. Professional and amateur producers should contact the nearest Concord Theatricals Corp. office or licensing partner to verify availability.

No one shall make any changes in this title(s) for the purpose of production. No part of this book may be reproduced, stored in a retrieval system, scanned, uploaded, or transmitted in any form, by any means, now known or yet to be invented, including mechanical, electronic, digital, photocopying, recording, videotaping, or otherwise, without the prior written permission of the publisher. No one shall share this title(s), or any part of this title(s), through any social media or file hosting websites.

For all inquiries regarding motion picture, television, online/digital and other media rights, please contact Concord Theatricals Corp.

MUSIC AND THIRD-PARTY MATERIALS USE NOTE

Licensees are solely responsible for obtaining formal written permission from copyright owners to use copyrighted music and/or other copyrighted third-party materials (e.g., artworks, logos) in the performance of this play and are strongly cautioned to do so. If no such permission is obtained by the licensee, then the licensee must use only original music and materials that the licensee owns and controls. Licensees are solely responsible and liable for clearances of all third-party copyrighted materials, including without limitation music, and shall indemnify the copyright owners of the play(s) and their licensing agent, Concord Theatricals Corp., against any costs, expenses, losses and liabilities arising from the use of such copyrighted third-party materials by licensees. For music, please contact the appropriate music licensing authority in your territory for the rights to any incidental music.

IMPORTANT BILLING AND CREDIT REQUIREMENTS

If you have obtained performance rights to this title, please refer to your licensing agreement for important billing and credit requirements.

YOU CAN SEE ALL THE STARS was commissioned by The John F. Kennedy Center for the Performing Arts and was first produced at the Kennedy Center American College Theater Festival in 2017.

CHARACTERS

ANABELLE MARTIN – (F/18) – a college student. English major. Brought a whole suitcase full of her favorite books with her to school. Loves things that are magic.

MARCY WELLS – (F/18) – a college student. Ana's roommate. A little ditsy, but good-hearted. Is taking astronomy, but hasn't picked a major yet.

KEVIN OBLANSKI – (M/19) – a college student. Roommate of Eddie Green. Smart, awkward, glasses. Doesn't know what to major in. Met Ana during Freshman Orientation, and they've been friends ever since.

KIM BARRINGTON – (F/20) – a college student. Beautiful, and spends time keeping herself that way. Girlfriend of the school's star quarterback Jesse Evans. Major: undeclared.

EDDIE GREEN – (M/19) – a college student. Football player. Offensive Lineman. Big, tough. An Engineering major who is trying to balance being serious about football, which is paying for his education, and actually getting one.

RONNI GRISSOM – (F/22) – a college student. Journalism major, who works on the school paper. A little bit intense. About everything.

SETTING

A college campus.

TIME

Now.

AUTHOR'S NOTES

The play moves quickly and seamlessly from place to place – including dorm rooms, the cafeteria, and the roof of Bromley Hall. More than one place should be able to exist on the stage at the same time – so that when we leave a dorm room, a character might remain sitting on his bed for a few moments, as the action begins in the next scene. There should be places outside the action, where a character might linger, until her next scene begins.

Ana should never leave the stage. This play belongs to her.

(The sky is full of stars, bright punctuation in the deep, black night.)

*(**ANA** stands on the edge of the roof, staring down into the darkness below.)*

(There is a long moment in which she stands there, precarious.)

(Perhaps there is a tearing sound... a bow wrenching violently against the strings of a violin. And we shift in time to the moments that led to this moment.)

*(The light changes. And without moving, **ANA** is now standing in the doorway of the dorm room she shares with **MARCY**. It is Sunday morning, seven a.m.)*

*(**ANA** is wearing a dressy skirt and blouse, but no shoes. She holds the front of her blouse closed with one hand, because two buttons have been torn from it, and one of her shoes in the other. She holds herself very still.)*

*(**MARCY** sits cross-legged on her bed, wearing sweats. She is eating a bowl of cereal and reading an astronomy book for class.)*

MARCY. I hope it was fun.

ANA. *(Beat.)* What?

MARCY. The party. I hope it was fun. It's, like, seven in the morning. You want some cereal?

ANA. *(Beat.)* No.

MARCY. I spent half the night on the roof.

*(**ANA** comes the rest of the way into the dorm room, and closes the door behind her. She stands there, by the door.)*

You can see all the stars from the roof of Bromley Hall. I am kind of loving Astronomy. Unexpected. I always sucked at science in high school. I guess I didn't realize there were so many, like, different ones. I am so not into Bunsen burners. Like, really. There was a fire. Did I ever tell you about that? Mr. Bruckner was so mad at me. The sprinklers went off. Bunsen burners are really not good. Telescopes, though...

*(**ANA** doesn't say anything; doesn't move.)*

*(**MARCY** looks up from her book.)*

Are you okay?

ANA. I don't know.

MARCY. You look...

*(A moment. **ANA** moves to go.)*

ANA. I'm going to take a shower.

MARCY. Hang on.

*(**ANA** pauses. She doesn't look at **MARCY**.)*

Where's your other shoe?

*(**ANA** looks down at the shoe in her hand.)*

ANA. I don't know.

(Beat.)

Maybe I dropped it.

> (**ANA** *takes three odd little sips of air. She drops the shoe. Then she grabs her bathrobe.*)

MARCY. Are you okay? Like, really.

ANA. I'm...

> (**ANA** *goes.*)
>
> (**MARCY** *looks after her, not sure what just happened.*)
>
> (*The light shifts. Time shifts.*)
>
> (**ANA** *moves into a pool of light at the edge of the stage.*)

Something happened last night.

> (*A moment.*)

I don't remember... exactly what. Something...

> (*Beat.*)

There was a party. I dressed up. I had drinks and dances and didn't think about the paper I'm supposed to be writing this weekend for Freshman Seminar, not once. I felt on top of the world, happy and warm and funny, and then... I wasn't. I knew where I was, then I didn't. I could move, then I couldn't.

> (*Beat; we hear the violent, desperate sound of wings beating against a window.*)

When I woke up there was a fluttering sound, like wings, like wings beating against the inside of my head, and a sweet red smell, and everything... hurt.

> (*Beat.*)

Everything hurts.

(**ANA** *puts the bathrobe on, belting it tightly around herself. She returns to the dorm room, which is empty now, and dark, and curls up in her bed. She pulls the blanket up over her.*)

(*The light shifts.*)

(*And it is Wednesday in the cafeteria. Voices and music* *and plates tap, tap, tapping against each other.*)

(**MARCY** *sets her tray down at an empty table, and sits. She has her earphones in, and doesn't see* **KEVIN** *until he taps her on the shoulder. She jumps.*)

MARCY. What?

KEVIN. Where's Ana?

(**KEVIN** *stands over* **MARCY,** *backpack slung over his shoulder, clothes rumpled, hair wild. He looks like he just rolled out of bed, but... he always looks like that.*)

(**MARCY** *pulls the earbuds out of her ears.*)

MARCY. She's in our room.

KEVIN. I knocked. She's not there.

MARCY. She's there. She's just not...

KEVIN. She's there?

MARCY. Quit standing over me.

(**KEVIN** *sits down across from* **MARCY.**)

---

* A license to produce YOU CAN SEE ALL THE STARS does not include a performance license for any third-party or copyrighted music. Licensees should create an original composition or use music in the public domain. For further information, please see Music Use Note on page 3.

KEVIN. Did I do something?

MARCY. I don't know. Did you?

KEVIN. I don't think so.

(**MARCY** *eats.*)

She wasn't in Seminar. Again. And she's not answering my texts.

MARCY. Maybe she doesn't like you anymore.

KEVIN. Cut it out.

(*Beat.*)

Is she sick?

MARCY. (*Beat.*) I don't know.

KEVIN. You live two feet away from her.

MARCY. She's been acting weird.

KEVIN. Weird how?

MARCY. I don't know.

KEVIN. Tell me!

MARCY. Sleeping all the time. Not eating.

KEVIN. Not eating?

MARCY. I've been bringing her back fruit and cookies, but they're just stacking up on her desk.

KEVIN. For how long?

MARCY. Since... Sunday morning.

(*A moment. Then* **MARCY** *takes a key on a lanyard out from around her neck, and puts it on the table.*)

She won't tell me what's going on. Maybe she'll tell you.

(**KEVIN** *picks up the key, and exits.*)

(The lights shift.)

*(And **KEVIN** is knocking on the door of **ANA** and **MARCY**'s dorm room ten minutes later.)*

KEVIN. *(Calling.)* Ana?

(A moment.)

It's me.

(Beat.)

It's Kevin.

(Beat.)

Are you there?

*(**ANA** stares out; awake, but not moving.)*

Papers were due in Seminar today. You were supposed to read mine and put in all the commas for me.

(Beat.)

Are you mad at me?

ANA. *(Calling out.)* Go away.

KEVIN. *(Beat.)* No.

(Pause.)

Marcy gave me her key, but I'm not going to come in if you don't want me to. But I'm not going to go away either.

(Beat.)

What's wrong?

ANA. Nothing.

KEVIN. I don't believe you.

(Beat.)

Are you sick?

ANA. No.

KEVIN. Are you...

(Beat.)

Did something happen?

*(**ANA** doesn't answer.)*

Is it your Grandpa?

ANA. Everything's fine.

KEVIN. Then come out here.

*(**ANA** doesn't answer.)*

Ana?

(A moment.)

I'm going to come in, okay?

(A moment.)

*(Then **KEVIN** pulls the key out of his pocket and opens the door.)*

*(**KEVIN** goes over to **ANA**, and sits on the floor beside her bed.)*

*(The scene in the dorm room continues as the light shifts, and **MARCY** steps into a pool of light.)*

MARCY. I don't know why she won't tell me what happened.

(Beat.)

We've only been roommates for two months. Maybe that's why. Maybe she needs more time to...

(Beat.)

The college put us together. It's like the first test, before classes even start. She's okay. She doesn't play music loud or anything. But we don't have anything in common. When she was unpacking, she had one whole box that was a series of dragon books. Hard cover. And I said, 'You're gonna read all those? There's movies you know.' And she didn't laugh. She just said, really serious, 'I like the books better.'

(Beat.)

I bring her bananas and oatmeal cookies I smuggle out of the cafeteria in my coat pockets. But she doesn't tell me what's going on.

(Beat.)

After I find out, I wish I didn't know. You know?

*(**MARCY** looks over at the dorm room, where **ANA** is sitting up in her bed, now, covers pulled up around her. **KEVIN** is still sitting on the floor.)*

KEVIN. You have to...

(Beat.)

You have to go to the cops. And the hospital. Or... both.

ANA. And say what?

KEVIN. That somebody...

(Beat.)

That somebody...

ANA. I don't even know what happened!!

(Beat.)

Except it won't stop bleeding. I'm still bleeding. My sheets are all...

*(**KEVIN** covers his face with his hands.)*

I'm sorry.

KEVIN.　Don't say that.

(Pause.)

Don't say that. You don't have to be sorry. He should be...

*(**KEVIN** smashes his fists on the floor over and over again.)*

*(**ANA** presses herself up against the wall.)*

ANA.　Stop doing that!!!

*(**KEVIN** stops, breathing hard.)*

KEVIN.　I'm sorry.

(A moment.)

Jesse Evans?

*(**ANA** looks away.)*

Tell me.

ANA.　He asked me to dance with him. And then he kept bringing me drinks. And then I don't... I don't... remember. I don't even know whose room it was I woke up in, some room, I was alone and it was dark and I was... it hurt, and I was... and I came back here and locked myself in.

(Beat.)

But I can't sleep, and I keep... bleeding, and it still hurts, so this morning I messaged him. 'What did you do to me?' Is what I said. And this is what he said.

(**ANA** *hands* **KEVIN** *her phone.*)

KEVIN. *(Reading off the screen.)* 'Shut up. You loved it.'

ANA. Kevin?

KEVIN. Yeah.

ANA. I didn't love it.

(*Beat.*)

I don't even remember it.

(**KEVIN** *clenches his fist.*)

(*The lights shift.*)

(**KEVIN** *gets up and walks into a pool of light.*)

KEVIN. I convince her to go to the health center, and to tell them what happened. And campus safety comes, and she tells them what happened. And in my head... in my head there's this kind of forty-two minute Law & Order episode kind of idea that we'd done what we were supposed to do and it would all get fixed. But I'm not right about that at all.

(*The lights shift, and it is three days later.*)

(**ANA** *stands in a pool of light, looking out. She's holding a crumpled piece of paper.*)

ANA. When you share what happened, everything gets worse.

(*Beat.*)

Nobody tells you that.

(Beat.)

I didn't know there could be something worse. But there is. Everyone looks at me. It's like I'm in a...

(Reaches out her hand.)

...zoo. A cage at the zoo. Everybody can see me and I can't get away.

(Pause.)

They didn't let Jesse play in the game last night. Because they're investigating. I guess they're...

(Beat.)

They're looking into it. Campus safety said they'd...

(Beat.)

Jesse wasn't allowed to play last night. And apparently that's my fault. Because I ...

(Beat.)

Not his fault? Because he...?

(Beat.)

You know how I know it's my fault?

*(**ANA** smiles wryly. She holds out the crumpled piece of paper. It reads: 'You mess with the team, we'll mess with you.')*

(She turns it toward herself. Looks at it.)

(Reads.)

'You mess with the team, we'll mess with you.'

(Pause.)

I don't have a team.

> (**ANA** *looks over at the dorm room that she shares with* **MARCY**.)

> (**MARCY** *stares at the door. The word 'SLUT' has been spray painted across it.*)

> (**ANA** *walks over to* **MARCY**, *and they look at the door together.*)

I'm sorry.

MARCY. You didn't spray paint the word 'SLUT' on our door.

> (**ANA** *looks at the floor.*)

I'll get some soap and paper towels.

ANA. Okay.

> (*Beat.*)

You can ask for somebody else if you want. To room with somebody else.

> (**MARCY** *goes and gets some soap and a roll of paper towels.*)

> (*The lights shift as she speaks.*)

MARCY. That doesn't seem right, though.

> (*Pause.*)

People are saying stuff about her now, all of a sudden. We're freshmen, nobody knows we exist, and suddenly I keep hearing her name. And I keep hearing what Jesse is saying about her, ever since he got benched.

(KEVIN steps forward, and provides the voice of Jesse Evans.)

MARCY.
'Why would I want to tap that?'

KEVIN.
'Why would I want to tap that?'

MARCY. ...he says.

MARCY.
'She's a whore,'

KEVIN.
'She's a whore,'

MARCY. ...he says.

MARCY.
'I can do whatever I want. I'm a football player.'

KEVIN.
'I can do whatever I want. I'm a football player.'

MARCY. ...he says.

(A moment.)

The notes shoved under the door and the notes written on the door are scary, because... we live here. But the pictures are worse. When the pictures start to go around, Kevin – Ana's geek friend Kevin – decides to have a talk with his roommate, Eddie, who's on the football team with Jesse.

(MARCY goes over to the door and starts to wash off the paint with ANA as the light shifts to KEVIN and EDDIE's dorm room.)

(KEVIN sits on the edge of his bed.)

(EDDIE is doing his before-bed exercise routine of sit-ups and push-ups.)

KEVIN. Hey.

(Beat.)

Hey. Eddie.

EDDIE. What did I say about talking to me?

KEVIN. Not to do it.

(*Pause.*)

Because we're just roommates, not friends. And you don't intend to be my friend. I'm not in your class. We're both freshmen, so I knew what you meant when you said that. And not to ask you for tickets to games or to use your name to get into parties I couldn't get into myself because I'm a geek. It was a totally off-the-charts awesome first day of college, meeting my new –

EDDIE. Stop talking! I'm doing my routine, and you're interrupting it.

KEVIN. You have to tell Jesse to stop.

(**EDDIE** *continues exercising, counting under his breath.*)

Eddie?

EDDIE. I don't have to do shit.

KEVIN. Maybe you're doing it, too. Sending them around to people.

(*Beat.*)

Are you doing it, too?

EDDIE. I don't know what you're talking about.

KEVIN. I'm talking about the pictures.

(**EDDIE** *continues exercising.*)

(**KEVIN** *takes out his cell phone, pulls up a picture, and holds it in front of* **EDDIE***'s face.*)

(**EDDIE** *smacks the cell phone out of* **KEVIN***'s hand. It goes sailing across the room, and clatters onto the floor.*)

She's my friend.

EDDIE. You have friends?

KEVIN. Not as many as you. Everybody loves you.

EDDIE. Not everybody.

KEVIN. You have a poster over your bed that says, 'Everybody loves me! I'm a football player!' It's, like, three times bigger than my *Doctor Who* poster.

EDDIE. My Mom got it for me for Christmas last year. Why am I talking to you?! Jesus.

(**EDDIE** *goes back to doing push ups, but* **KEVIN** *pushes* **EDDIE** *over with his foot.*)

KEVIN. How would you feel if it was your friend that the whole school was exchanging pictures of, naked, covered in vomit, unconscious, getting fucked in the –

(**EDDIE** *leaps up and grabs* **KEVIN**, *pressing him up against the wall.*)

How would you feel if it was you?

(**EDDIE** *slams* **KEVIN** *against the wall.*)

(**KEVIN** *closes his eyes, but then opens them again.*)

Someone sent her a text message today that said if she didn't take back what she said happened, they were going to cut off her tits with a deer knife.

(**EDDIE** *holds* **KEVIN** *there for a moment, then lets go of him.*)

*(**KEVIN** slides down the wall until he's sitting against it.)*

*(**EDDIE** grabs his team jacket, and moves toward the door.)*

What kind of person are you?

*(**EDDIE** glances at **KEVIN**, then goes.)*

(The lights shift.)

*(**KEVIN** steps forward, into the light.)*

Ana mostly stops going to her classes. But on Wednesday, she goes to her Psych class, because Jesse's girlfriend, Kim, is in it. Ana thinks that maybe if she talks to Kim, Kim will make Jesse, and whoever else is sending the pictures and the threats, stop. I try to talk her out of it, because I've met Kim, and she's…

(Beat.)

Well…

(The lights shift. And we're in a classroom on Wednesday afternoon, a week and a half after what happened.)

*(**ANA** sits at the desk in front of **KIM**, turned around to face her, and they are already mid-conversation.)*

KIM. He said you were asking for it.

ANA. Asking for it.

KIM. Wanted it.

ANA. I was unconscious.

KIM. Before you were unconscious.

ANA. I wasn't... I wasn't... I wasn't 'asking for it' before I was unconscious. I didn't want it after I was unconscious.

KIM. Why did you dance with him?

(*A moment.*)

Why did you –

ANA. Because he asked me. Because I like to dance. Because –

KIM. Because he's all that, and you're nothing.

ANA. I'm not nothing.

(*A moment.*)

I'm not.

(*A moment.*)

KIM. You know where I was?

ANA. Where you...?

KIM. My grandma's funeral. I flew home for my grandma's funeral. I'm gone for five minutes, and some skank comes after my boyfriend.

ANA. I'm not –

KIM. I forgave him.

ANA. (*Pause; incredulous.*) For raping me?!

(*Pause.*)

He raped me.

(*Pause.*)

Kim, he raped me.

KIM. (*With finality.*) I don't believe you.

(**KIM** *moves toward the door.*)

ANA. He took pictures. He took pictures, and he's sending them around to everyone.

KIM. That's what you get for being a lying skank.

> (**KIM** *slides her bag over her shoulder, and leaves.*)

> (**ANA** *stands there for a moment, watching* **KIM** *go.*)

> (*The light shifts.*)

> (**ANA** *walks into her dorm room, and writes on the wall – the beginning of a list of things that she feels like she's done wrong, that she will continue to write over the course of the play.*)

> (*She writes, 'I shouldn't have gone to the party.' And 'I shouldn't have been drinking.' And 'I shouldn't have danced with him.'*)

> (*The lights shift.*)

> (**KIM** *looks out, defiantly.*)

I've invested a lot of time and effort into Jesse. Him and me being together. We're great together. Perfect. We're perfect together. And I'm not going to let anybody screw that up. Not her. Not even himself.

> (*Pause.*)

I don't actually forgive him.

> (*Pause.*)

I have to, so I do. I act like I do. I forgive him with all the parts of me that anybody sees, including him, because I have to, because... But there's a small part of myself that nobody will ever know about that's so goddamn angry I could burst into flames.

> (**KIM** *walks into the library, where* **EDDIE** *has a bunch of papers and his Engineering textbook spread out on a table. He's working through some equations, trying to figure something out.*)

Hey. Eddie.

> (**EDDIE** *looks up, and then gazes warily at* **KIM.**)

What are you doing here?

EDDIE. Studying. Trying to study. I have a test. What do you want? Jesse's not here.

KIM. I want to talk to you.

EDDIE. We don't have anything to talk about.

KIM. The cops are talking to everybody who was there. At the party.

EDDIE. Yeah.

KIM. You have to tell them you were with Jesse the whole time and he didn't do anything.

> (**EDDIE** *laughs.*)

EDDIE. That's what you want to talk to me about?

KIM. They've already benched him for Sunday's game and tomorrow's game.

EDDIE. I know.

KIM. They could arrest him or something.

EDDIE. Maybe they should.

KIM. That wouldn't be good for any of us.

(Beat.)

He's the best. On the team. He's the best, and we're winning because of him.

EDDIE. I know.

KIM. We lost on Sunday because he wasn't there.

EDDIE. Yeah.

KIM. So tell them you were with Jesse the whole time. And he didn't do anything.

*(**EDDIE** tries to do another equation.)*

Eddie!

EDDIE. No.

KIM. No what?

EDDIE. I'm not saying that.

KIM. Why not?

EDDIE. Because I wasn't with him the whole time. And he did do something.

KIM. You don't know that.

EDDIE. Yeah, I do.

(The lights shift.)

*(**KIM** disappears as **EDDIE** stands up, and steps away from the library.)*

Football saved me, when I was in high school. Gave me discipline. It gave me a place when I didn't have a place. The team – being part of a team. And now I'm supposed to go against all that? Now I'm supposed to stand up for some chick I never even met, over the guys I spend every single day with? Why?

(Beat.)

Why?

(The lights shift.)

*(**ANA** stands alone in her dorm room.)*

(She writes, 'I shouldn't have trusted Jesse.' on her wall. She writes, 'I shouldn't trust anyone.' She writes, 'I don't trust anyone.' She turns and speaks.)

ANA. There are consequences to coming forward and saying what happened to you.

(Beat.)

My father can't look at me. My mother just wants me to come home. When Jesse is benched for a third game, the threats get worse. Some talk show host on the radio says I'm lying and gives out my phone number. I can't sleep, but I keep missing classes because time has started to get really slippery and strange, slow and fast.

(Beat.)

And then I get a visit from the Assistant District Attorney. The one in the gray suit and the high heels who said she was 'looking into' what happened to me.

*(**MARCY** steps out onto the stage, providing the voice of the Assistant District Attorney.)*

MARCY.	ANA.
'We don't have enough evidence at this time to pursue the case against Jesse Evans...'	'We don't have enough evidence at this time to pursue the case against Jesse Evans...'

ANA. She says.

MARCY.	**ANA.**
'We don't have enough evidence at this time.'	'We don't have enough evidence at this time.'

ANA. She says.

MARCY.	**ANA.**
'We don't have...'	'We don't have...'

    (**ANA** *shakes her head.*)

ANA. Because I didn't...

MARCY. 'Come forward right away.'

ANA. Because I couldn't...

MARCY. 'Give us specific details about what happened.'

ANA. Don't you believe me?

MARCY. 'It isn't about believing you or not believing you.'

ANA. It felt like it was, though.

    (Beat.)

I couldn't...

    (Beat.)

I was...

    (Beat.)

Alice. Through the looking glass. I couldn't...

    (A moment.)

So what do I do now? Drop out of school, like my mom wants? Change schools, like my dad wants, to some place closer to home? Stay, but let it go? How do I do that? Stay, and fight? I don't know how much more fight I ...

(**ANA** *turns, and writes on her wall, 'What am I supposed to do now?')*

It feels like I'm at a tipping point.

(Beat.)

Precarious.

(Beat.)

Everything is precarious right now.

(Beat.)

I'm holding onto the rope with both hands, but the ground is giving way underneath me. Anything could happen.

(The sound of wings against windows.)

(**ANA** *presses her hands against her ears, to try to block it out. When that doesn't work, she flees.)*

(The lights shift.)

(And we're two days later, in **KEVIN** *and* **EDDIE***'s dorm room. They are both sitting on their beds, earphones in.* **KEVIN** *is watching something on his laptop.* **EDDIE** *is looking at* **KEVIN**. **KEVIN** *notices.)*

KEVIN. What?

(**EDDIE** *shakes his head. Looks down at his homework. But then looks at* **KEVIN** *again.* **KEVIN** *takes out his earphones. So does* **EDDIE**.*)*

What?

EDDIE. Nothing.

KEVIN. Fine.

 (**KEVIN** *begins to put his earphones back in, but stops when* **EDDIE** *speaks.*)

EDDIE. How is your, uh... friend?

 (*A moment.*)

KEVIN. Ana.

EDDIE. Yeah.

 (*The scene between* **EDDIE** *and* **KEVIN** *continues, but on the other side of the stage, in her dorm room,* **ANA** *writes on the wall.*)

 (*'I'm afraid all the time.' 'My hands won't stop shaking.' 'I can't take this anymore.'*)

KEVIN. *(Pause.)* She's considering dropping out of school, because even after changing her phone number, she's still getting threats. And the D. A. decided not to prosecute Jesse, because of a lack of evidence, so he's going to classes again, and playing again. Which makes her feel like...

 (*Beat.*)

... I don't even know.

 (*A moment.*)

 (*Then* **EDDIE** *speaks. His words are provocative, but the way he says them is tentative... he's trying to figure something out.*)

EDDIE. Maybe she's a whore.

KEVIN. Maybe you're an asshole.

EDDIE. No... but really, maybe –

KEVIN. What does that even mean?

EDDIE. Maybe she wanted it.

KEVIN. While she was unconscious?

EDDIE. She was dancing with him earlier.

KEVIN. Dancing implies consent to being –

EDDIE. Maybe.

> (**KEVIN** *shoots a look at* **EDDIE.**)

Okay, no.

> (*Pause.*)

You don't even know what happened.

KEVIN. No.

EDDIE. This could ruin Jesse's LIFE.

KEVIN. <u>Jesse's</u> life?

EDDIE. He's a football player.

KEVIN. Yeah.

EDDIE. He's the only reason we're winning this year.

KEVIN. Why are we even... talking about football?! It's not about fucking football. Why is everything at this fucking school about fucking football?

EDDIE. It is, though.

> (*Pause.*)

People will go crazy if he gets kicked off the team. They'll be so mad. My dad drives one hundred and eighty miles to see every game.

KEVIN. Didn't he miss your Engineering presentation last week?

EDDIE. *(Beat.)* Some things are important. Some things aren't.

> *(A moment.)*

KEVIN. Why do you want to know how Ana is?

EDDIE. *(Beat.)* I don't know.

> *(The lights shift as **EDDIE** moves out of the dorm room, and looks out.)*

I don't know why I want to know, but I want to know. How she is.

> *(**EDDIE** turns, and looks over at the cafeteria.)*

> *(**ANA** sets a tray on the table, but then just stares at the plate of food in front of her, not eating.)*

> *(**KEVIN** joins **ANA** at the table.)*

I go to the cafeteria one day, and just watch her. Kevin comes by and tries to get her to eat something, but she just sits there with her back to the wall, looking at everybody like they're wolves or something. He tries to touch her hand, but she pulls her hand away, like she can't stand for anybody to touch her.

> *(Pause.)*

I keep thinking what a rotten way that would be, to go through the world feeling like.

> *(**EDDIE** and **KEVIN** both exit.)*

> *(A moment.)*

> *(Then **RONNI GRISSOM** approaches **ANA**'s table. Sits down beside her.)*

RONNI. Hi.

ANA. *(Pause.)* Hi.

> *(Pause.)*

You're in my chemistry class.

RONNI. Ronni. Grissom. Yeah.

ANA. Did you need something?

RONNI. I work for the Pen and Sword.

> (**ANA** *looks blankly at* **RONNI**.)

The newspaper. The school newspaper.

> (**ANA** *gets up.*)

Don't go.

> (**ANA** *pauses.*)

I want to talk to you. About what happened to you.

ANA. How do you... how do you know what –

RONNI. Someone group-texted me a picture.

ANA. Oh, God.

RONNI. I recognized you. From class.

> (**ANA** *moves away, toward the door, leaving her tray.*)
>
> (**RONNI** *gets up and follows* **ANA**.)

ANA. Stop following me!

RONNI. Will you please just listen?

ANA. Why doesn't anyone hear me when I say no?!

> (**RONNI** *stops.*)

You can't stop people from sharing my picture. You can't keep me from seeing... seeing... seeing him at random moments when I leave my room, which makes me not want to leave my room, ever. You can't make the police department prosecute him.

RONNI. They aren't going to prosecute him?

ANA. Shut up!

(Beat.)

You can't stop me from going over that night in my head, over and over, trying to figure out…

(Beat.)

I have a list. On my wall. Of all the things I did wrong. I'm up to fifty-three.

(Pause.)

I don't know why I just told you all that.

*(**RONNI** moves closer to **ANA**, tentatively. Carefully.)*

RONNI. Because you need to tell someone.

(Pause.)

It's the job of the journalist to seek truth and report it.

(Pause.)

I know I just work for the school newspaper, but… I take that shit seriously. Ana.

(Beat.)

Your name is Ana, right?

(Pause.)

I've spent three and a half years here, learning about serious journalism and writing about the fucking Powder Puff Ball after the fucking Civil War game.

(*Beat.*)

When I got your... when I got that picture, I thought, look at that poor girl, why isn't somebody writing about <u>that</u>?

(*Beat.*)

Then I thought, why aren't <u>I</u> writing about that?

(*Beat.*)

Because I've been at this school for three years, and your picture isn't the first one I've gotten.

(*A moment.*)

Can I come and talk to you?

(*Pause.*)

If you say no, I'll never bother you again.

(*Pause.*)

Please say yes.

ANA. (*Pause.*) Yes.

(*The lights shift.*)

(**RONNI** *and* **ANA** *sit across from each other.* **RONNI** *has a legal pad in front of her, and a pen in her hand. She turns on a recorder, and sets it on the table.*)

RONNI. Ronni Grissom, interviewing Anabelle Martin. Monday, ten a.m.

(*Pause.*)

Anabelle...

ANA. Ana. People call me Ana.

RONNI. Ana. Tell me a little bit about yourself.

(**ANA** *smiles oddly, a strange expression crossing her face.*)

What is it?

ANA. That question.

RONNI. *(Beat.)* Tell me a little bit about yourself?

ANA. I'd begun to forget that I'm... like... a whole person. A real person. Not just someone something happened to.

(Pause.)

I'm from a small town called Blue River.

(Beat.)

It's more of a muddy brown, really.

(Beat.)

That's a town joke.

(Pause.)

I don't know what to say.

RONNI. What do your parents do? In Blue River?

ANA. My dad drives for UPS. Which means he works fifteen hour days all through December and falls asleep after presents on Christmas. My mom is an accountant. Part time. My brother is still at home. He's eleven.

(Beat.)

We're a pretty regular sort of family.

(Beat.)

They're strict, but they love me. They want me to come home. We're not telling my brother, but I think he knows anyway.

RONNI. It's hard to keep things secret nowadays.

ANA. Yeah.

RONNI. What's your major?

ANA. English. It might change, but...

(*Beat.*)

I like books.

RONNI. You want to write them?

ANA. No. I don't know. I like to read. Fantasy and science fiction, mostly. No, don't write that down. It will make me sound like a geek.

RONNI. How did you end up at that party?

ANA. I shouldn't have gone.

RONNI. I didn't say that.

(*Pause.*)

You're in college now. You're supposed to go to a party or two.

(*Pause.*)

You're a freshman, right?

ANA. Yeah.

(*Pause.*)

A few of us went together. From my dorm. We were supposed to...

RONNI. (*Beat.*) Look out for each other?

ANA. It's not their fault I was...

RONNI. *(Gently.)* Is it hard to say the word?

ANA. Raped.

> *(Beat.)*

I can say it.

> *(Beat.)*

Maybe this isn't a good idea. Maybe I should just... shut up. Disappear.

RONNI. You have as much right to be here as anybody else. To be here at this school, and not to be hurt or threatened. What happened to you wasn't fair. It wasn't right, and it wasn't fair, and somebody should be put in jail for it, and instead –

ANA. – he hasn't even been arrested.

RONNI. Don't the pictures prove anything?

ANA. They're just of me. They're just of...

> **(RONNI** *tries to put her hand on* **ANA***'s shoulder, to reassure her, but* **ANA** *pulls away.)*

(Quickly.) My hands still shake sometimes. I still can't eat sometimes. I have trouble going out the door sometimes, especially after dark. People still look at me. Really. I'm not imagining it. They look at me, when they know. And when someone new comes around, who doesn't know, I don't know how to tell them.

> *(Pause.)*

I don't... um... feel safe anymore. Ever. I don't trust my own judgement anymore. Which is a bitch. I don't ever want to let anybody touch me ever again. And... you know... all that doesn't bode well for me ever being able to...

(**ANA** *puts her head down on her arms.*)

(**RONNI** *looks out.*)

RONNI. She stays there two more hours and talks to me. My recorder runs out of battery. For half the time, I find myself holding her hand, even though we never knew each other before all this.

(*Beat.*)

I cry when I write it all up. Then I wonder what kind of journalist I am. We're supposed to be objective.

(*Beat.*)

But I'm not a machine. I'm writing this story because I care about it. Her. Ana. What happened to her. Her sitting there telling me what happened to her was the… the bravest thing I've ever seen.

(*Pause.*)

And then they kill my story.

(*The lights shift.*)

(**ANA** *is in her dorm room, with* **MARCY.**)

(*We see* **RONNI** *call* **ANA** *on her cell phone, from outside the newspaper office.*)

(**ANA** *looks at her phone, and answers it when she sees that it's* **RONNI.**)

ANA. Hey.

RONNI. Hey, Ana.

(*A moment.*)

ANA. What's up?

RONNI. I ...uh...

> *(A moment.)*

ANA. Just tell me.

RONNI. They quashed my article.

ANA. Who did?

RONNI. The university. The 'powers that be.' Our faculty advisor tried to argue with them, but they wouldn't...

> *(Pause.)*

They said it's to protect you. Your privacy.

> *(A long moment.)*

I'm sorry.

ANA. Yeah.

RONNI. Ana...

> *(**ANA** hangs up.)*

> *(**RONNI** shoves her phone back into her pocket.)*

What I ask the 'powers that be,' the president of the university, when I write him a letter about this, is 'what do you think you're teaching me by doing this? By suppressing the truth about what happened here at this college, by supporting a rapist more than you support his victim? What do you think I'm learning about how the world works?'

> *(**RONNI** exits.)*

> *(**ANA** sits there, in her dorm room, on her bed, staring at her phone.)*

> *(**MARCY** looks over at her.)*

MARCY. You okay?

ANA. I wish everybody would quit asking me that.

    *(**MARCY** looks back at her laptop.)*

They're not going to run the story. In the school paper.

MARCY. I thought you didn't care about the story.

ANA. *(Beat.)* I don't.

    (Beat.)

It doesn't matter.

    (Beat.)

It really doesn't matter. Right?

    *(**ANA** gets up.)*

You still have your telescope set up, upstairs?

MARCY. Yeah. On the southwest corner. I put tape over the lock. And a lawn chair. It's great.

ANA. You can see all the stars from the roof of Bromley Hall.

MARCY. Yeah!

    (Beat.)

Don't break it. My Aunt Susie gave me the telescope for my birthday.

    *(**ANA** leaves.)*

    *(The lights shift. And we are in **KEVIN** and **EDDIE**'s dorm room.)*

    (The two of them are in the same position they were in earlier – sitting on their beds, earphones in.)

(**EDDIE** *is looking at* **KEVIN** *again.*)

KEVIN. What?

EDDIE. I don't have money for college. I get to be here because I play football.

KEVIN. Okay.

EDDIE. If I don't play football, I don't get this whole future they've been promising. I have to go home and be nothing.

KEVIN. Those are not the only two choices.

EDDIE. Right now, it feels like the only two choices.

KEVIN. You've been thinking about what I said. About Ana.

(*A moment.*)

EDDIE. Yeah.

(*Pause.*)

I have to tell you something.

(*Beat.*)

I never shared any of those pictures of... of Ana.

KEVIN. Okay.

(*Beat.*)

Good.

(*Beat.*)

What do you want me to say?

EDDIE. Shut up a minute.

(**KEVIN** *does, but* **EDDIE** *doesn't speak.*)

KEVIN. What do you want to tell me?

EDDIE. I was there. At the party. I was drinking. Everybody was drinking. The music was really loud. Mostly I was just hanging out with Taft and Otter, but at some point I went upstairs to try to find a bathroom. Somebody had totally taken over the downstairs bathroom. I opened a door, and...

KEVIN. Oh, my God.

EDDIE. I saw them. Jesse and... Ana. And she was... she was totally out, unconscious, but he was...

　　　(Beat.)

What kind of thing is that, to do to a person? I mean... what kind of thing?

　　　(Beat.)

And I thought that then, even though I was really drunk. I thought, 'What kind of thing is that, to do to a person?' But I didn't... I didn't do anything to stop it. I didn't even say anything, I just...

　　　(Pause.)

But I will now.

KEVIN. You'll –

EDDIE. Tell. Testify. Whatever. Say what I saw.

　　　(Beat.)

He still has her shoe. One of her shoes. She lost it when he was...

　　　(Beat.)

He has it in his locker.

　　　*(**KEVIN** rubs his face, then looks up at **EDDIE**.)*

KEVIN. You want me to drive you?

EDDIE. Drive me?

KEVIN. To the police station.

EDDIE. *(Beat.)* Yeah.

KEVIN. The D. A. won't be there until morning.

EDDIE. I'm not going to change my mind.

KEVIN. Okay.

> *(The lights shift, and we are alone with **ANA**
> up on the roof.)*

ANA. Everything feels broken. Even time. It's all too much.

> *(Beat.)*

Time doesn't just go in one direction any more. For a long while, I go backwards more than I go forwards. I drift in time, I lose time, I stick in time…

> *(A moment.)*

Sometimes I'm stuck in <u>this</u> moment.

> *(**ANA** puts her hands up, and shakes them
> near her ears, and we hear the sound of wings
> beating against windows.)*

Sometimes I'm stuck in <u>this</u> moment.

> *(The light shifts. And we are precarious with
> **ANA**, on the edge of the roof of Bromley Hall,
> like we were at the beginning of the play.)*

And I'm so tired of being stuck.

> *(The sky is full of stars. **MARCY** was right.
> You can see all the stars from here. But **ANA** is
> looking down into the darkness below.)*

> *(**MARCY** appears, suddenly, on the roof. She
> looks across at **ANA**.)*

(She understands the precariousness of this moment, but doesn't know what to do about it.)

MARCY. I have a problem with you.

ANA. *(Beat.)* Yeah?

MARCY. Yeah.

(A moment.)

I want you to stop writing what you think you did wrong on our walls.

ANA. Yeah?

MARCY. They're my walls, too.

ANA. I know.

MARCY. You should write what <u>he</u> did wrong on <u>his</u> walls instead.

*(**ANA** turns and looks at **MARCY**.)*

(A moment.)

ANA. That's a really good idea.

MARCY. I know. I'm really smart.

*(**ANA** laughs.)*

*(**MARCY** smiles at **ANA**.)*

Stop standing so close to the edge. You'll fall off.

(A moment.)

You should listen to me.

ANA. Because you're really smart.

MARCY. Yeah.

> (**ANA** *takes a breath. Then steps away from the edge. She sits down, cross-legged, and looks up at the stars.*)

> (**MARCY** *moves closer to* **ANA**. *Sits down near her, in her lawn chair.*)

Celestial navigation.

ANA. What?

MARCY. Celestial navigation. Is what we're studying now? In Astronomy. It's where you figure out where to go by the stars. Like ships did. People on ships. Before, you know, GPS was on everybody's phone. Before everybody had a phone. Before phones existed.

> (*Pause.*)

Polynesian sailors had songs they'd sing that were like maps. Map songs. That said when to turn, at which constellation. The sailors who'd gone between the islands before sang the songs, and then the young sailors would learn them and know where to go.

> (*Pause.*)

We listened to a recording, of people singing one of the songs.

ANA. I bet that was nice.

MARCY. It was.

> (*Beat.*)

I came up here to tell you I think your story in the paper is important, and it sucks that they're not going to run it, and we should print it out and just, like, hand it out to people.

ANA. It doesn't matter.

MARCY. It does, though.

(Pause.)

How does the next person navigate this if you don't share how you did?

ANA. That's not my problem.

MARCY. But it's something you could do.

ANA. I'm not navigating it very well.

MARCY. You're still here.

(A moment.)

(Then **ANA** *leans back, so she's resting her head against* **MARCY***'s legs.* **MARCY** *runs her hand over* **ANA***'s hair in an odd, reassuring little gesture of support.)*

*(***KEVIN** *bursts through the door, onto the roof. He sees* **ANA** *and* **MARCY** *sitting there.)*

KEVIN. Ana!

*(***ANA** *looks over at* **KEVIN***.)*

Eddie's going to testify.

ANA. *(Beat.)* What?

KEVIN. He... he saw what happened that night. And he's going testify.

ANA. He saw?

(A moment.)

Oh.

KEVIN. They'll have to prosecute now.

ANA. I don't know.

KEVIN. I think they will.

ANA. Even if there's a trial, that won't fix anything.

MARCY. You're not broken.

ANA. I'm a little broken.

(Pause.)

But I'm still here.

*(**ANA** stands up.)*

(With sudden determination.) Want to help me do something? Both of you.

(Beat.)

It involves paint. And a printer.

*(**ANA** and **MARCY** go to their dorm room and paint over the words that **ANA** has written on their walls.)*

*(**RONNI** hands a stack of paper with her interview with **ANA** printed on it to **KEVIN**, who hands a copy to **ANA**. **ANA** looks down at the paper, then steps forward and speaks.)*

In March, I'm suspended for a week after painting 'Jesse Evans raped me. Why is he still allowed to go to school here?' on the wall of the football stadium. During alumni week. And handing out a thousand copies of the interview I did with Ronni.

*(**KEVIN**, **MARCY** and **RONNI** chime in.)*

KEVIN, MARCY & RONNI. We help.

*(**ANA** lets the paper fall.)*

ANA. And I go talk to Eddie.

(The lights shift.)

(**ANA** *looks across the stage at* **EDDIE,** *who is alone at a table in the cafeteria, eating lunch.*)

(**ANA** *goes over to* **EDDIE.***)*

Hi.

(**EDDIE** *looks up, then freezes when he sees that it's* **ANA.***)*

(*A moment.*)

Can I sit down?

EDDIE. Yeah.

(**ANA** *sits down across from* **EDDIE.***)*

(*A moment.*)

ANA. You're not playing football anymore.

EDDIE. No.

(*A moment.*)

I don't know what to say to you.

ANA. You don't have to say anything.

(*Pause.*)

I hate you for not stopping him.

(**EDDIE** *looks down at his plate.*)

That's not what I came over here to say.

(*A moment.*)

Thank you for telling the D. A. what you saw.

EDDIE. I should have done something.

ANA. Yeah.

(Pause.)

You did do something.

EDDIE. Pretty late.

ANA. Yeah.

(Pause.)

But you did it.

(A moment.)

EDDIE. How are you still going to school here? After everything?

ANA. How are you?

(A moment.)

EDDIE. *(With difficulty.)* I'm sorry.

*(A moment. Then **ANA** nods.)*

*(**ANA** stands up, and steps away from the table in the cafeteria...)*

ANA. I still think about... for a long time I'd think about the roof of Bromley Hall.

*(And suddenly **ANA** is standing in both places at once – still in the cafeteria with **EDDIE**, but also up on the roof of Bromley Hall.)*

EDDIE. What does that mean?

(Pause.)

The roof of Bromley Hall.

ANA. Jumping off it. I think about...

(**ANA** *takes a step toward the roof of Bromley Hall, and the cafeteria space, and* **EDDIE,** *fade into the darkness.)*

(**KEVIN** *and* **MARCY** *are on the roof.* **KEVIN** *drinks a soda,* **MARCY** *looks through her telescope, and* **ANA** *– not so close to the edge now – speaks.)*

Talking to Eddie, painting the wall, sharing my story... It didn't change anything, but it did. Just like the trial... just like the trial didn't change what happened, but it changed... I don't know. Something.

(*Beat.*)

Something changed.

(*Beat.*)

I made something change.

(*Pause.*)

Celestial navigation.

(**ANA** *smiles.)*

(*A moment.*)

The hardest thing is to stay.

(*Beat.*)

It's really hard to stay.

(*Beat.*)

But I'm staying.

(**ANA** *joins* **MARCY** *and* **KEVIN** *by the telescope. The three of them gaze up at the* *sky together. The stars continue to shine overhead. Enduring.*

End of Play

A FEW STATISTICS

The White House Task Force to Protect Students from Sexual Assault released their first report in April 2014, leading with the following statistic: one in five college students experiences sexual assault during their college career.

Over half of sexual assaults committed against college students involve alcohol, according to researchers at Wayne State University.

The American Civil Liberties Union (ACLU) estimates that 95% of U.S. campus rapes go unreported.

Approximately two out of three sexual assaults are committed by an attacker that the victim knows, according to the Rape, Abuse, and Incest National Network (RAINN).

Survey results published by RAINN show that about 60% of victims do not go to police, and only 25% of reported assaults actually lead to an arrest.

(Statistics are collected from http://www.bestcolleges.com/resources/preventing-sexual-assault/)